POLLY AND THE PRIVET BIRD

For Carol and Peter, John and Jenny,
John and Janet, Anne, Annich and Noel,
Tim and Meryl

A Red Fox Book

Published by Random House Children's Books
20 Vauxhall Bridge Road, London SW1V 2SA

A division of the Random House Group
London Melbourne Sydney Auckland
Johannesburg and agencies throughout the world

First published by Hutchinson Children's Books 1990

Red Fox edition 1992

Printed and bound in Belgium by
Proost International Book Production

ISBN 0 09 980900 1

POLLY AND THE PRIVET BIRD

Story by Ann Cartwright

Illustrations by Reg Cartwright

RED FOX

T here once was a lady called Polly who talked to flowers.

'Good morning, lupins,' she would say in her bright sing-song voice. And they would stretch tall and proud to the sun.

'Don't worry,' she'd say to the daffodils and tulips when they had stopped flowering, 'I'll see you again next year.'

The grown-ups thought Polly was strange and kept away from her house on the hill. The children knew differently. They loved Polly's garden which seemed to have a magic of its own.

One morning Polly looked at her privet bush and sighed. It had grown so wild and unruly that it threatened to smother all the flowers. Polly decided to do something about it before it smothered her.

'From that untidy bush I will make a fine bird,' she said.

She fetched her ladder and shears from the garden shed and set to work. Snip, snip, snip went the shears until a head appeared. Snip, snip, snip they went and soon the bird had a beak and a neck.

All day long the shears snipped away the hours until the sun sank low and disappeared behind the trees. As night fell Polly snipped her last snip, climbed down and stood back to look at her work.

A magnificent privet bird stood silhouetted against the evening sky.

Next morning, as soon as Polly was washed and dressed, she rushed outside to look at her privet bird. 'My word, you'd think it was real,' she said, climbing up on its back.

Just then she heard a noise. From far, far away came the sound of children crying.

'Come, come, my beauty,' she cooed to the bird. 'There's work for us here.' And she kept on talking, soft and low, all the while stroking the bird's neck.

Was it the wind that rustled the leaves? No, with a shake and shudder the privet bird lifted its proud head, spread its wings and soared into the air like a beautiful green aeroplane. Polly looked about her in amazement as they flew higher and higher, and higher still across fields and meadows, until they reached the river that ran from the village to the town.

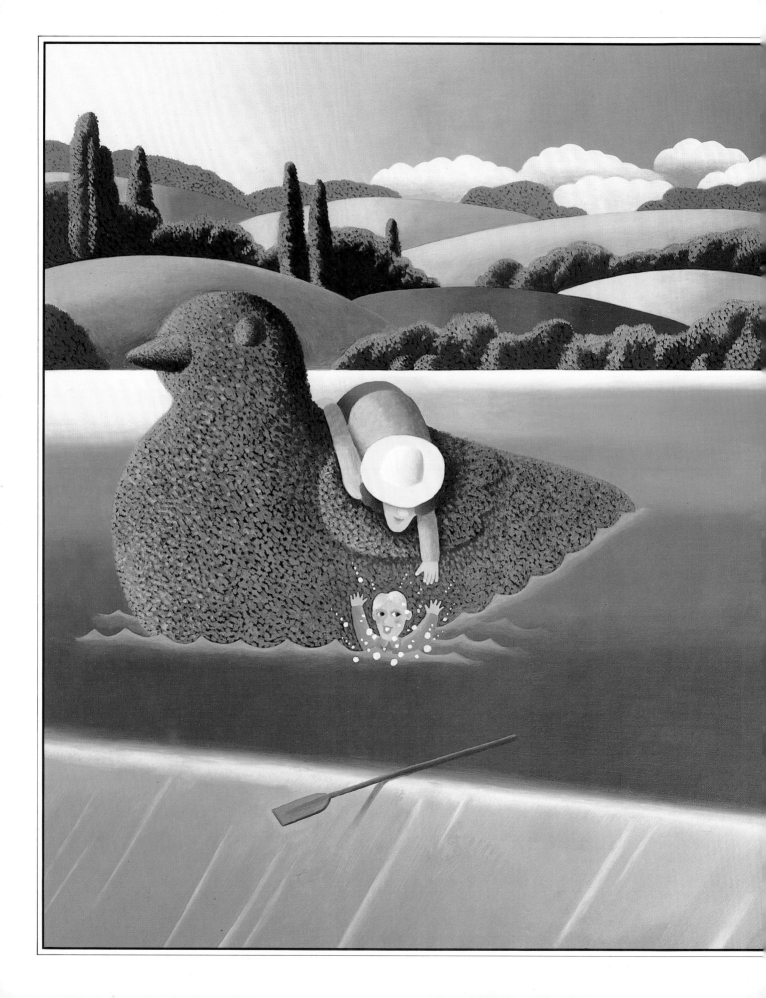

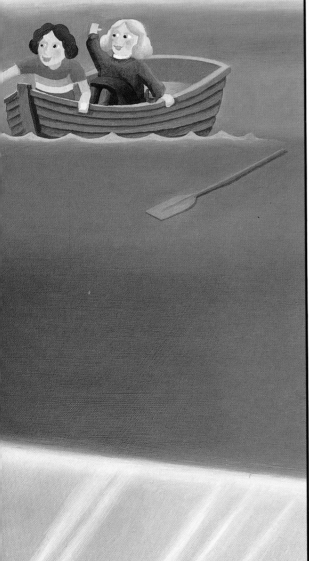

A boat drifted loose on the water. Two children cried and cried. Their little brother had fallen in and was being carried fast downstream by the current.

'Quickly, carefully, my beauty,' said Polly. Down swooped the privet bird, landing gracefully on the water with hardly a splash.

One by one, Polly gathered up the children and placed them carefully on the privet bird's back. 'Prepare for take off!' she cried.

Away they flew, across the fields and meadows, over the village and back to Polly's house.

After a fine tea of toast and honey, the children set off down the hill, their eyes wide with wonder.

Back at home, the children told everyone about their adventure.

'Privet bird indeed!' laughed the grown-ups. 'Whatever will you think of next?'

One night the wind turned wild and a great storm got up. So ferocious was the wind that the trees blew down and blocked the roads and railways. So fierce was the rain that it swelled the river until its banks burst and the fields were flooded.

Next morning the whole village was nothing but an island in a lake of rain. The children could not get to school and the parents could not get to work.

Everyone was hungry, but there was no food to be had for it had floated out of the village shop and away.

From her house on the hill, Polly heard the cries of the village in trouble. She put on her Wellington boots and once again spoke to the privet bird. 'Come, come fine strong bird,' she said. 'We're needed once more.' And she whispered and cooed until the heart of the privet bird began to beat. Again it rose from its leafy perch and soared up into the sky.

On and on they flew until day turned into dusk and they reached the big supermarket on the edge of the town.

Polly parked the privet bird and began to shop. She bought bread and orange juice and cornflakes and porridge. She arrived back at the village just as night was turning into day.

That morning each household found a fine breakfast sitting on the windowsill. And the same thing happened every morning until the river finally went down and the shop opened up its doors.

At last the people could venture out.

'I wonder who brought our breakfasts,' said the grown-ups. 'It's a mystery. Perhaps it was a helicopter, or a boat.'

At that very moment the fluttering of leafy wings sounded overhead.

'Look, *look!*' cried the children. 'There's the answer.'

But the grown-ups just carried on talking and never even bothered to look up.

'Well, if they won't look they won't see,' said the children. So they put their thoughts in their pockets and kept the magic to themselves.

Then, one bright windy morning, the postman was out delivering letters when he gasped in astonishment. At first he thought a tree had uprooted itself and taken flight. But as it came closer there was no mistaking the great leafy bird which flew across the road and disappeared over the top of the hill.

Straight away, he rushed back to the village with his extraordinary tale. As the grown-ups listened, their mouths fell open and their eyes popped with astonishment. For weeks they talked of nothing but Polly and her privet bird. Could it really be true? And the more they talked about it the more they decided that it was.

'You must thank her,' said the postman.

'About time,' said the children.

And the whole village marched through the meadow and up the hill to Polly's house.

The garden was as lovely as ever. The roses, gladioli and geraniums basked in the late summer sun. But where the privet bird had stood, stately and proud, there was a tangle of untidy leaves.

'Why its nothing but an old privet bush,' scoffed the grown-ups. 'How silly we've been.' And they laughed at themselves for believing such an unlikely story.

'Well, if they won't believe, they won't know,' said the children to Polly.

Polly smiled. 'One day I shall oil and sharpen my shears and make another bird,' she said softly.

And the whole garden, from the blades of grass to the tall proud hollyhocks, sighed with pleasure.